The Tortoise and the Hare

Dona Herweck Rice

Assistant Editor
Leslie Huber, M.A.

Editorial Director
Dona Herweck Rice

Editor-in-Chief
Sharon Coan, M.S.Ed.

Editorial Manager
Gisela Lee, M.A.

Creative Director
Lee Aucoin

Illustration Manager/Designer
Timothy J. Bradley

Cover Art and Illustration
Chad Thompson

Publisher
Rachelle Cracchiolo, M.S. Ed.

Teacher Created Materials
5301 Oceanus Drive
Huntington Beach, CA 92649
http://www.tcmpub.com
ISBN 978-1-4333-0290-9
©2009 Teacher Created Materials, Inc.
Reprinted 2012

The Tortoise and the Hare

Story Summary

Tortoise and Hare live in the woods with all their animal friends. Hare loves to hop and run very fast. It always boasts that it is the fastest and best in the woods. The other animals know that Hare is fast. But they think Hare's boasting is annoying. Tortoise decides to do something about it. Tortoise challenges Hare to a race. Hare thinks the challenge is silly.

Can slow-and-steady Tortoise beat faster-than-fast Hare? Read the story and you will find out.

Tips for Performing Reader's Theater

Adapted from Aaron Shepard

- Don't let your script hide your face. If you can't see the audience, your script is too high.

- Look up often when you speak. Don't just look at your script.

- Talk slowly, so the audience knows what you are saying.

- Talk loudly, so everyone can hear you.

- Talk with feelings. If the character is sad, let your voice be sad. If the character is surprised, let your voice be surprised.

- Stand up straight. Keep your hands and feet still.

- Remember that even when you are not talking, you are still your character.

- Narrator, be sure to give the characters enough time for their lines.

Tips for Performing
Reader's Theater *(cont.)*

- If the audience laughs, wait for them to stop before you speak again.

- If someone in the audience talks, don't pay attention.

- If someone walks into the room, don't pay attention.

- If you make a mistake, pretend it was right.

- If you drop something, try to leave it where it is until the audience is looking somewhere else.

- If a reader forgets to read his or her part, see if you can read the part instead, make something up, or just skip over it. Don't whisper to the reader!

- If a reader falls down during the performance, pretend it didn't happen.

The Tortoise and the Hare

Characters

Narrator	Hare
Blue Jay	Tortoise
Frog	Porcupine

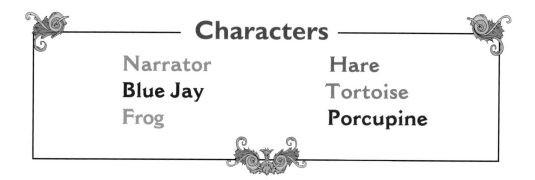

Setting

This reader's theater takes place in the woods. The woods are home to many animals. They are filled with trees, plants, and flowers. A long dirt trail runs through the woods.

Act I

Narrator:	The sun has risen over the woods. Noisy Blue Jay cries out. It wakes the animals from a restful sleep.
Blue Jay:	Heeere! Heeere! Wake up! Wake up!
Frog:	Yawn! Is it morning already? Ribbit!
Hare:	Quiet down, will you? A speedy hare like me needs its rest.
Tortoise:	But a tortoise is always happy to wake up and greet the sunrise. Good morning!
Narrator:	Hare just wrinkles its nose. Hare doesn't care about the sunshine when it can be sleeping instead.
Blue Jay:	It *is* a nice morning, Tortoise. But sleep is nice, too.

Narrator: Blue Jay worries when the animals argue. Blue Jay tries not to make anyone angry.

Frog: I agree! I agree!

Narrator: And Frog tends to agree with everyone.

Hare: Will you two pipe down? I can't sleep. You should want to take care of me. After all, I am the fastest and the best. Nothing can bring you greater joy than seeing me comfortable and happy.

Tortoise: What a grumpy bunny! You don't know what you're missing. How can you just laze around when there is a great day ahead of you?

Frog: Yes, how can you laze around?

Hare: How? Just watch me! I'll show you how, you old slowpoke.

Frog: Hare will show you, you old slowpoke!

Narrator: And with that, Hare falls back to sleep. But the other animals begin to work and play. They are ready to enjoy the day.

Act 2

Porcupine: Hello there! What are all of you doing?

Tortoise: We are starting the day, old friend. I am glad you are here, Porcupine. You can enjoy the day with me.

Porcupine: I would have been here sooner, but you know how slow I can be.

Tortoise: I don't mind slow! Fast or slow, I am glad to see you.

Blue Jay and Frog: Me, too!

Porcupine: And I am glad to be here. What do you want to do today?

Tortoise: If I had my way, I would put that Hare in its place. Hare is so crabby and boastful!

Porcupine: Well, what can you do? Hare is very fast.

Frog: I agree! I agree!

Porcupine: And you are very slow.

Frog: That's true! That's true!

Blue Jay: Yes, you are wise, Porcupine.

Tortoise: Yes, Hare is fast. But Hare is lazy, too. Hare is just a little too big for its britches. I think it's time that Hare learned a lesson.

Frog: I agree!

Blue Jay: Be careful what you are saying, Tortoise!

Porcupine: What lesson?

Tortoise: "Slow and steady" just may know a little more than "fast and lazy"!

BlueJay and Frog: Ooooo.

Porcupine: Are you sure you know what you're doing?

Tortoise: Just watch!

Act 3

Narrator: Tortoise marches over to Hare and wakes it up. Hare is not happy about it.

Hare: What are you doing? Can't you see that I am sleeping?

Tortoise:	Oh, I can see that. But I have a challenge for you. Do you think you can handle it?
Hare:	Ha! Are you joking? I am the fastest and the best, remember? Just try me. There's nothing you can do that I can't do better.
Blue Jay and Frog:	Ooooo.
Tortoise:	All right. Here it goes. I challenge you to a race through the woods. We follow the trail. No cheating! No help from anyone! We race on our own legs.
Narrator:	Hare can barely keep from laughing.
Hare:	A race? Between you and me? My powerful hind legs in a race against your stubby turtle feet? A race of speed? Oh, you're on, slowpoke.
Tortoise:	Then we have a deal, Hare? Tomorrow morning, bright and early, we race. Deal?

Hare:	Oh, ho ho, it's a deal!
Narrator:	With that, they shake hands. And Hare falls back asleep.

Act 4

Narrator:	The sun rises the next morning. All the animals wake up, except Hare.

Song: Are You Sleeping?
(Frère Jacques)

Hare:	Why are you fools singing? Can't you see that I'm sleeping? Don't you understand the importance of my beauty sleep?
Blue Jay:	Oh, don't be mad!
Frog:	Yes, don't be mad!

Tortoise: It's time for our race, Hare. Remember?

Hare: Race smace. You don't have a chance. I only have to *think* about racing, and I can beat you. Go away and let me sleep now. I can win with my eyes closed.

Narrator: And that's just what Hare does. Hare closes its eyes and goes back to sleep.

Blue Jay: Oh, my. Hare stayed up too late last night.

Frog: That's true. Hare stayed up very late.

Narrator: Just then, Porcupine arrives, slow as ever.

Porcupine: Am I too late for the race? I came as fast as I could.

Tortoise: You are in plenty of time, friend. It is a beautiful day. I am rested and ready to go.

Porcupine: But where is Hare?

Blue Jay: Sleeping. Oh, dear.

Frog: Yes, sleeping.

Tortoise: We tried to wake Hare, but it yelled at us.

Porcupine: Then I say, "Let the race begin!"

Narrator: All the animals gather around the starting line. Tortoise takes its place. Blue Jay tries once more to wake Hare. But Hare tells Blue Jay to go away.

Hare: Scram!

Blue Jay: Okay, okay!

Frog: Ribbit!

Narrator: The animals do as Hare asks and leave it alone. They get ready for the race. Porcupine starts things off.

Porcupine: On your mark. Get set. Go!

Narrator: Tortoise takes off slowly. Tortoise is a tortoise, after all.

Tortoise: What a nice day for a brisk walk!

Blue Jay: Go, Tortoise, go!

Frog: Yes, go as fast as you can!

Tortoise: I will!

Narrator: And Tortoise does. Tortoise walks as quickly as its four legs can go. After some time, Tortoise and the other animals disappear around a bend in the road. It is then that Hare wakes up and looks around.

Hare: Yawn! Stretch. Hmmm. Where has everybody gone? Oh, yes, that silly race. Guess I'd better take a look.

Narrator: Hare puts on its running shoes and jogs around the bend. Hare soon catches up.

Hare:	Ha! Some race. Just look at you! Do you see how quick I am?
Narrator:	Hare dances around Tortoise.
Tortoise:	Yes, I see you. But I am not worried.
Hare:	You make me laugh, Tortoise. Ha ha! I am going to lie down under this tree and laugh for awhile. Ha ha! Hee hee!
Narrator:	And that is exactly what Hare does. But Tortoise keeps on racing, slow and steady.

Act 5

Narrator:	The sun passes through the sky. Tortoise has been racing all day. Now, Tortoise is near the finish line. And Hare is just waking up.

Blue Jay: Hooray for Tortoise! I knew you could do it all along.

Frog: Yes, I knew you could do it!

Porcupine: We all did! Good for you!

Tortoise: Thank you, friends. I am giving it my best. I am slow, but I am steady, too.

Hare: Yawn. Stretch. What's all that noise?

Narrator: Hare looks around in confusion. Hare spots Tortoise near the finish line.

Hare: Oh, no! That silly race!

Narrator: With that, Hare jumps up and starts to run.

Hare: Watch out! Here I come!

Blue Jay: Oh, here comes Hare! I knew you could do it, Hare! I mean Tortoise. I mean Hare. Oh, dear.

Frog: Yes, I knew you could do it!

Narrator: Yes, Hare might have done it. But in its hurry, lazy Hare forgets to tie its shoelaces. Hare doesn't know it is in danger. Hare runs as fast as it can. Hare comes nearer and nearer to Tortoise.

Hare: Ha ha! I knew I would beat you!

Tortoise: Slow and steady, slow and steady.

Blue Jay: Yes, slow and steady!

Frog: Slow and steady!

Porcupine: Keep going, Tortoise, slow and steady!

Hare: You're fools! No tortoise can beat a hare in a race. Ha ha!

Tortoise:	Maybe a tortoise has never won before. But I am not worried. Slow and steady, I say.
Hare:	Ha ha! Hee hee!
Narrator:	Sadly for Hare, it laughs too soon. While running fast to catch up, Hare steps on its shoelace. Hare falls flat on its face! Hare is just inches from the finish line, but Hare does not cross it.
Porcupine:	Too bad for you, Hare. I knew you could do it, Tortoise!
Narrator:	And with that, Tortoise crosses the line.
Porcupine:	Tortoise wins the race!
Hare:	What?!
Blue Jay, Frog, and Porcupine:	Hooray!

Tortoise: That's right, Hare. I have won. Fast and lazy is not the way to be.

Hare: But how? But why? I am Hare. I am the fastest and the best.

Tortoise: You may be fast, Hare.

Blue Jay: So fast!

Frog: Yes, so fast!

Tortoise: Yes, you are fast, Hare. And I am slow. But slow and steady always wins the race.

Poem: What If the Score Is Against You?

What If the Score Is Against You?

Anonymous

What if the score is against you,
And you know defeat is sure?
Keep giving your best.
Defeat is a test
To see if you can endure.

Come in on your feet at life's ending,
And the past will seem full and fine.
There's a healthy glow
Only doers can know
In the spurt at the finish line.

Are You Sleeping?
(Frère Jacques)

Traditional

Are you sleeping,
Are you sleeping,
Brother John,
Brother John?
Morning bells are ringing.
Morning bells are ringing.
Ding ding dong!
Ding ding dong!

Frère Jacques,
Frère Jacques,
Dormez vous,
Dormez vous?
Sonnez les matines.
Sonnez les matines.
Din, din, don!
Din, din, don!

Glossary

big for its britches—thinks too highly of itself

boastful—bragging

brisk—quick and lively

crabby—annoyed and easily made angry

defeat—loss; not winning

endure—to last; keep going

hare—a type of rabbit with long ears and long back legs especially good for jumping

hind—back; rear

laze—rest lazily

spurt—big push of energy

tortoise—a land turtle

woods—large, thick area of trees; part of a forest